To the kids at Bright Beginnings,

Best wishes on all your colorful
& vibrant aquatic adventures!

J. P____

To my wife Kathryn.
I love you more than ice cream.

Sea Skunks

Copyright © 2020 by Josh Potler

Illustration by Josh Potler & Garon Levine

Printed in the United States of America

ISBN: 978-0-578-82227-3

The sea was calm. The sun was shining and the Skunks looked forward to another beautiful day out on the water.

The old boat wasn't much, but the skunks did not need anything fancy, for they were used to spending time simply enjoying the nature that surrounded them.

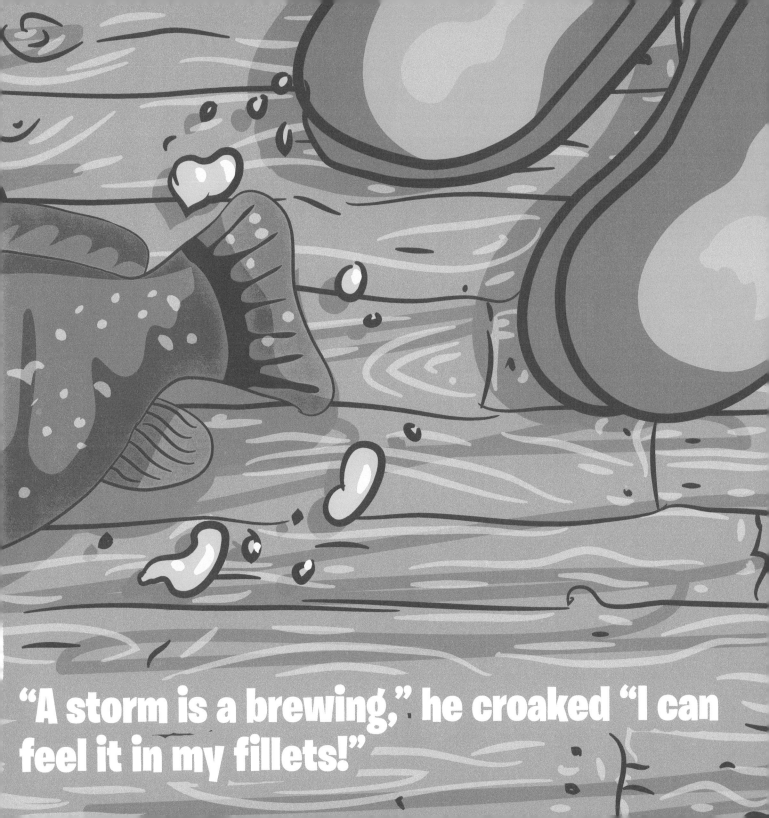

"A storm is a brewing," he croaked "I can feel it in my fillets!"

Warned with the news, the Skunk Squad guided Gilbert back into the sea and began preparing the boat!

"Lock the latches!" - Check!

and, "Wrap the ropes!" - Check!

The storm came and blew and blew. The rain dumped in droves, but the skunks were safe deep down in the hull of the old boat.

When the wind stopped and the rain had ended, Stinkers, Smelly and Stench climbed out on to the deck to see what they could see.

Stinkers spoke and the other two listened. "We will use our special skunk spray to save our ocean friends and clean up the trash that has been stirred up in the storm!" he said.

The skunks agreed that now was the time for the three to become real Sea Skunks!

The skunk squad suited up with masks and fins, wetsuits, and snorkels, and jumped overboard to save Tony and Sienna.

In moments, the squad surged across the surface of the water bound towards freeing their friends!

Stinkers untangled Tony from the plastic drink rings! Smelly bumped the bucket and Sienna swam free! Stench began collecting the plastic particles that had gathered after the gale.

Once everyone was swimming smoothly, Sienna offered a tour of her home to give thanks for her riveting rescue!

The Sea Skunks were thrilled and dove down to follow her as she led them through her tropical treasure trove, her residence on the reef.

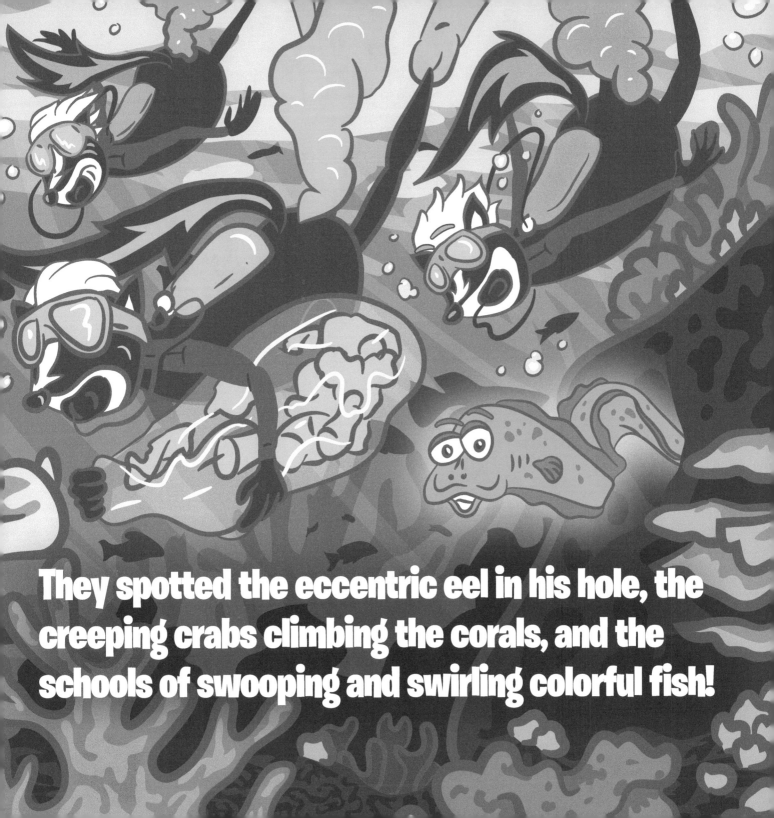

They spotted the eccentric eel in his hole, the creeping crabs climbing the corals, and the schools of swooping and swirling colorful fish!

Back on the boat after retrieving the rubbish, the skunk squad threw away the trash and dried off after quite a dazzling day.

The three were thrilled the litter had been lifted and promised to protect the sea from the plastic permanently.

With their friends swimming soundly and the sea safe again, the three were off to bed to snuggle in their cozy cabin with dreams of the ocean and their next adventure, as the welcoming waves whisked them to sleep!

CPSIA information can be obtained
at www.ICGtesting.com
Printed in the USA
BVHW020252260521
607105BV00002B/18